I Want a Pony

Jeanne Betancourt

illustrated by Robert S. Brown

SCHOLASTIC

SYDNEY AUCKLAND NEW YORK TORONTO LONDON MEXICO CITY
NEW DELHI HONG KONG BUENOS AIRES PUERTO RICO

Scholastic Australia Pty Limited
PO Box 579, Gosford NSW 2250
ABN 11 000 614 577
www.scholastic.com.au

Part of the Scholastic Group
Sydney ● Auckland ● New York ● Toronto ● London ● Mexico City
● New Delhi ● Hong Kong ● Buenos Aires ● Puerto Rico

First published by Scholastic Inc. in 1994.
This edition published by Scholastic Australia in 2005.
Text copyright © Jeanne Betancourt, 1994.
Illustrations copyright © Scholastic Inc., 1994.
Cover design copyright © Scholastic Australia, 2005.

Reprinted 2005, 2006 and 2007 (twice), 2008

All rights reserved. No part of this publication may be reproduced or
transmitted in any form or by any means, electronic or mechanical,
including photocopying, recording, storage in an information retrieval
system, or otherwise without the prior written permission of the
publisher, unless specifically permitted under the Australian
Copyright Act 1968 as amended.

National Library of Australia Cataloguing in Publication data
Betancourt, Jeanne.
    I want a pony.
    For middle primary children.
    ISBN 978-1-86504-741-6.
    1. Ponies - Juvenile fiction. I. Brown, Robert S., 1953- .
    II. Title. (Series : Betancourt, Jeanne. Pony pals ; 1).
813.54

Printed by McPherson's Printing Group, Victoria.

10 9 8 7 6   8 / 0

For my pal, Leslie

The author thanks Elvia Gignoux for generously sharing her lifelong knowledge and love of horses.

Thanks also to Dr. Kent Kay for medical consultation on this story.

Contents

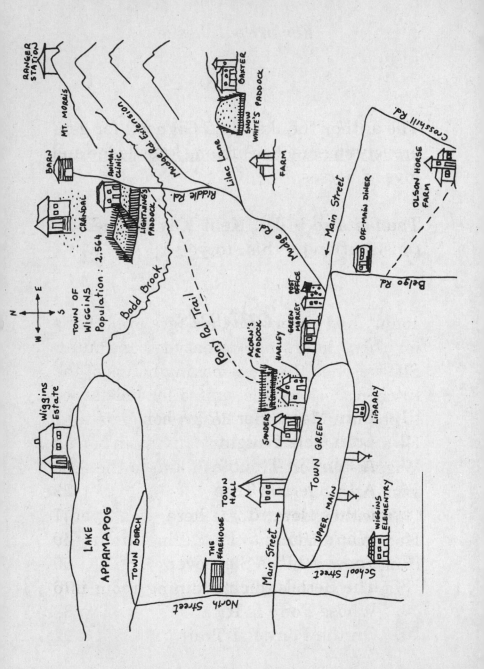

Lulu Meets Her Neigh-*bor*

Lulu had been at her grandmother's for three hours and twenty-two minutes. She watched the slow-moving hands of the kitchen clock as she waited for her father to phone and say that he'd made a mistake. He'd tell her that instead of living in boring Wiggins she could go with him to the Amazon jungle in Brazil.

"Lucinda, dear. Come here, won't you?" Her grandmother was calling from the front parlor.

Lulu ran through the dining room into

the parlor. The large sunny room, facing Main Street, wasn't a regular parlor. It was a beauty parlor: *Sanders Beauty Salon.*

Grandmother Sanders was squirting a pile of silver-gray curls with hair spray. Looking at Lulu's reflection in the chrome-framed mirror she said, "Lucinda, dear, we do not run in the house. It's not ladylike."

Lulu sneezed from the irritating hair-spray fumes.

"Well, now," the pile of silver curls said, "so this is your granddaughter?"

"Yes, indeed," Grandmother said. "Mrs. Cassarra, this is Lucinda Sanders. Lucinda, this is Mrs. Cassarra."

To Lulu, Mrs. Cassarra said, "How do you do?" To Grandmother, she said, "I can't imagine suddenly having a child to raise. At our age."

"I'm only here until my dad finishes his job in Brazil," Lulu informed her. "He's raising me."

"That's right," Grandmother told Mrs. Cassarra. "And I love having my grand-

2

daughter with me. As for my age, well, I have more energy at seventy than I did when I was younger." She looked at Lulu. "Now wouldn't a cut and a permanent do wonders for Lucinda's hair?"

Even though three mirrors showed that Lulu's brown shoulder-length hair was straight and stringy, she thought her hair was just fine. She hated the idea of spending even five minutes in the stuffy, smelly beauty parlor. Now if Grandmother had pony stables, she thought, I wouldn't mind those strong odors one bit.

The phone rang.

"Would you get that, Lucinda, dear?" grandmother said.

Lulu answered the phone by saying, "Sanders Beauty Salon."

"Lulu!" the voice on the other end exclaimed. "How's my girl?"

"Dad! I was waiting for you to call. I'm going to the kitchen phone to talk."

As Lulu ran back through the dining room, she reviewed how she would plead with her father to let her go with him to the Amazon. Maybe he already realized he'd made a mistake in not taking her. Maybe he was calling to tell her that.

But Lulu's father hadn't changed his mind. "Now about your allowance," he said. "I've wired the entire amount to the bank. But, remember, it's twenty-five dollars for each week."

"Dad, there's only one diner in this town and no toy stores or anything like that. There isn't even a movie theater. What am I going to spend money on?"

"Lulu," he responded, "think of living in Wiggins as an adventure. Go exploring and study nature. We always do that when we hit a new place."

"Grandma's too strict. She won't let me do anything. I know it," Lulu said.

"I survived her," he laughed.

"Yeah, but you're a boy. She's going to expect me to do all these girl things."

Her father's final words on the subject were, "Lulu, you're a strong, independent girl. You'll be okay. Listen, they've started boarding my plane to Brazil, so let's say good-bye. I know you'll have a great time in Wiggins. I love you."

"Bye, Dad. I love you, too," Lulu said, and hung up the phone.

As Lulu got into bed that night she thought about her father. She missed him very much. And she felt lonely for her mother who had died when Lulu was four.

Trying not to be sad, Lulu thought about her past two years in England with her father. Two afternoons a week, rain or shine, she attended a riding school where she took lessons on a Welsh pony named Ginger. On Ginger, Lulu had learned to walk, trot, canter, gallop, and jump. She became such a good rider that she and her friend Emily were allowed to take the school's ponies on long trails through the English countryside.

Lulu fell asleep picturing Ginger's sprightly trot, her laughing eyes, and the proud sound of her neigh.

A few hours later Lulu woke from a deep sleep with a start. Why was she hearing the sound of pony hooves on stone, and a pony's whinny? I must have been dreaming about Ginger, she thought. But as Lulu sat up in bed and rubbed her eyes to wake herself more, she heard her grandmother shouting, "Catch that horse! Get it before it destroys everything in my garden."

"He jumped the fence, Mrs. Sanders," a man's voice shouted. "But we'll catch him. Don't you worry."

Lulu ran to the window. Grandmother's yard was brightly lit by the outdoor lights. Lulu looked down at a scene of wild confusion. A man in red pajamas, a woman in a yellow bathrobe, and a curly blonde-haired girl in a pink nightgown were all scurrying around the yard trying to catch a shaggy brown pony.

To avoid his pursuers the pony was running across grandmother's stone patio.

The girl shouted, "Stop, Acorn. Please, stop."

A big clay pot of geraniums crashed to pieces on the patio. As the pony stopped to sample the geraniums, Lulu rushed out of her room and down the back stairs.

By the time Lulu reached the backyard the geranium-munching pony had been caught by the girl. Lulu thought the girl looked about ten years old, just like her. The girl was talking softly to the pony as she slipped a halter on him.

The girl led the pony to Grandmother and stopped in front of her. "I'm really sorry," she said. "I'll make it up to you."

"How can you, Miss Harley?" Grandmother asked angrily. "These are the last blooms of the season. Now they're ruined. There must be a law about keeping a horse in the backyard."

"Acorn's not a horse, ma'am," the girl said proudly. "He's a pony." She led Acorn onto the driveway.

Lulu wanted so much to talk to the girl and ask her about her pony. But with Grandmother so angry, Lulu knew it

wasn't the right moment to meet the neighbors.

Later, for the second time that night, Lulu fell asleep thinking about a pony. This time she thought of the bold and confident little Shetland pony who lived next door. Acorn, she told herself, I'm glad to have you as a neighbor. Tomorrow I'll pay you a visit.

Lulu Gets Caught

One look at the backyard the next morning and Lulu knew that the Shetland pony's midnight visit hadn't been a dream. She got dressed and went down the back stairs to the kitchen.

Her grandmother was already at work in the beauty parlor. Lulu made herself a bowl of cereal with slices of banana. Then she went into the backyard to clean up the mess that the pony had made. Lulu figured that if Grandmother's yard looked neat, she wouldn't be so angry at the neighbors.

First, Lulu picked up the pieces of broken clay pots. While she worked she snuck looks at the Harley backyard. She was hoping to see Acorn. But all she saw was a big vegetable garden and a three-sided shed with some bikes and a lawn mower. As far as she could tell there wasn't any place to keep a pony at the Harleys'.

Then she heard Acorn's whinny. She realized that the Harleys' yard was deeper than her grandmother's. The enclosed area that was Acorn's paddock was separated from the Harley vegetable garden by a row of bushes. Lulu ran to the far end of Grandmother's yard. There, between the shrubs and the fence, she had a good view of Acorn, his paddock, and a wooden shelter.

When the small pony saw Lulu, he stopped in his tracks and stared at her. Lulu held up one of the mangled red geraniums and called his name. Acorn's shaggy black mane bounced around his head as he ran up to the fence. He was coming at such a fast pace that Lulu was

11

afraid he'd jump like he had the night before. But the pony, seeing that the geranium was held out on his side of the fence, came to an abrupt halt. In a swift, bold motion he grabbed hold of the flower with his mouth and pulled it out of Lulu's opened hand.

"You are so cute," Lulu said. Then, remembering that Shetlands can be proud creatures, she added, "You're more than cute, Acorn, you're really handsome." She stroked his cheek. He nuzzled her shoulder. Then he turned and ran off across his paddock. In the middle of the field, the pony turned and bobbed his head at Lulu, as if to say, "Aren't you coming?"

Lulu heard the Harleys' back screen door rattle shut. A girl's voice called out, "Acorn. Acorn."

Quickly Lulu squatted out of sight behind the shrub. From this hiding place she watched the Harley girl walk across the paddock toward her pony. Acorn, rather than running over to the girl, trotted in the other direction. "Come and get me," he seemed to be saying as he bounded around the field.

For a while the girl played along with Acorn's game of tag. After a few minutes and an apple bribe, the girl had a halter on Acorn and was leading him to his shelter. There she brushed him and checked his hooves. Lulu knew this meant that the girl would soon be saddling him up for a ride.

Lulu watched as the girl put a bridle on Acorn, placed a saddle on his back, tightened the girth, and pulled down the stirrups. Finally, the girl led Acorn toward a gate at the far corner of the paddock. She opened the gate and then mounted her pony. Oh, how Lulu longed to be mounting a pony herself!

When she saw that the girl and Acorn were riding into the woods beyond the paddock, Lulu decided to trail them.

In a flash she hopped the fence and ran behind the row of maple trees edging the paddock. But by the time Lulu ran through the gate, Acorn and his rider were out of sight. Lulu saw that the only place they could have gone was on a narrow trail that snaked into a dense woods.

Lulu wasn't afraid of woods or forests. She'd been on lots of nature expeditions and camping trips with her father. And trailing animals was just the sort of thing she and her father did all the time. It was one of the things he'd be doing this year in the Amazon jungle.

After what Lulu estimated to be a mile on the trail, the woods opened onto a large sun-drenched field. Acorn stopped and the girl dismounted.

Lulu hid behind a big pine tree. She heard the girl say, "Here we are, Acorn. Look, there's Lightning. She's coming over to say hi."

Acorn whinnied and another pony whinnied in return. After a quick peek to see if the coast was clear, Lulu darted to a bush at the edge of the field. From there she saw a beautiful chestnut pony that was quite

bigger than Acorn. The pony was galloping across the field to meet a tall dark-haired girl and a dog who had just entered the paddock.

"Hi, Anna! Hi, Acorn!" the taller girl called. "What a great day!"

"It might be great for you," Anna replied in a discouraged voice.

When the other girl and her pony reached Anna she asked, "What's wrong? Is Acorn okay?"

"Pam, he jumped out of his paddock again last night. And that mean woman next door yelled and yelled like Acorn was some wicked animal. My mom and dad are really mad at me."

As Pam gave her pony loving pats on the neck, Lulu thought about how lucky Anna and Pam were to have their own ponies and a private trail to connect their two houses and paddocks. She was daydreaming about riding a pony on that beautiful woodland trail herself when she saw that the dog was running toward her hiding bush. He barked at the bush.

"What is it, Woolie?" Pam shouted.

"Shush, Woolie," Lulu whispered.

But Woolie barked even louder.

"I think he's found something," Lulu heard Pam tell Anna. "Let's go see what it is."

In an instant Lulu considered her options. She could jump up and say, "Hi, I'm Lulu Sanders. Just thought I'd introduce myself." Or, she could make a run for it.

She made a run for it.

"Hey," she heard Anna shout, "that's the girl staying next door."

"Why are you spying on us?" Pam yelled.

Lulu reached the trail and kept running.

Back in Grandmother's kitchen, Lulu walked in circles to slow down her breathing and keep her legs from cramping. She felt like such a jerk. Now, if she saw those girls it would be so embarrassing. And in a town the size of Wiggins she was bound to bump into them sooner or later. Especially since one of them lived next door. And they probably both went to Wiggins Elementary School. They might be in the fifth-grade class that she'd be joining on Monday. I'm the new girl in school, Lulu thought, and I've made a total fool of myself before I've even met anybody.

Well, she decided, at least I won't see Anna and Pam this afternoon — because I'm going on a hike.

Lulu put a sandwich, a canteen filled with water, three cookies, an apple, and two carrots into her backpack. She folded a piece of paper, found a pencil stub, and stuck those in the pocket of her jeans.

Before going into the beauty parlor to tell Grandmother that she was going on a picnic and hike, Lulu remembered to brush her hair and pull it neatly back with a barrette.

Grandmother was in the middle of giving a pretty red-haired woman a permanent. When Lulu told her that she was going on a hike, Grandmother looked alarmed.

"Dad and I always go for hikes when we get to a new place, Grandma. It helps us get our bearings."

"Well, stick to the roads," Grandmother said. "And make a map as you go so you'll be sure to find your way back."

"Of course," Lulu said. "Dad taught me that, too."

"Indeed," Grandmother said. "And who do you think taught him?"

Lulu smiled at the thought of her father as a little boy in Wiggins.

A Pony in Trouble

Lulu headed east down Main Street. After passing two blocks of shops and houses she came to a corner where Main Street met Mudge Road. She leaned against a tree and began her map by drawing and labeling lines for the streets. Then she walked on Mudge Road.

Soon Lulu came to another intersection. To her right she saw rolling hills of squared-off fields in different shades of green and brown. Some were dotted with black-and-white cows. The only buildings she could see were a white farmhouse and two red barns on the nearest hill.

A winding dirt road led into this landscape. A faded wooden sign told Lulu it was called Lilac Lane. After Lulu added Lilac Lane to her map, she took a deep breath of the crisp fall air and headed down the road.

As she walked along, Lulu found herself thinking what a great road Lilac Lane would be for riding a pony. After about a half mile the road took a sharp turn. Lulu figured she would come upon another farm and more cows. But when she turned the corner, there was only one animal in the squared-off field beyond the bushes — a white pony. She couldn't believe her eyes.

"Pony!" she called excitedly. "Look at you. You're so beautiful."

The pony was munching grass at the far end of the field. Hearing Lulu's voice, the pony looked up. Lulu walked over to the barbed-wire fence and called out, "Come here, let me get a better look at you. I bet that you're a Welsh pony."

Lulu noticed a yellow house next to the paddock. She decided that was where the pony's owner lived. But right now there were no cars in the driveway or any other signs that the people were home.

Lulu saw that the pony was still watching her. She reached into her backpack, took out an apple, and held it up for the pony to see. "I have a treat for you," she said. That was all the encouragement the pony needed. The pony ran across the paddock in a direct line to where Lulu stood.

"You know what," Lulu told the pony. "I think this is the perfect spot for my picnic."

The pony gently pushed at Lulu's shoulder with its nose, as if to say, "Where's that apple?"

Lulu was worried that the pony would get hurt on the barbed wire. To encourage the pony to move away from the fence, Lulu reached over it and offered the apple in her open hand. The pony gently took the apple with her teeth, then backed away to savor the juicy treat.

Lulu dropped her backpack into the paddock. She carefully raised the top barbed-wire strands, making just enough space to climb through into the field.

As Lulu stood up in the paddock, she saw that the pony had already eaten the apple and was now snorting around at her backpack. Lulu rubbed the smooth white slant of the pony's neck to get her attention.

"Hey, pony," she said, "I've got some more treats for you — but unless you can work a zipper you'd better let me do the unpacking."

Lulu looked into the pony's face. "You're a sweet thing," she said. "But look at all those burrs sticking in your mane. After lunch I'll pull them out. If I had a brush, I'd give that white coat of yours a good grooming, too."

The pony's ears pointed straight up to the blue sky, and her big brown eyes looked right at Lulu. The pony seemed to be saying, "I was really lonely. It's so nice to have company. Now, what's in that feed bag of yours?"

While Lulu ate her sandwich and cookies she fed the pony a carrot. Then she poured water from the canteen into her cupped hand so the pony could have at least a few licks of water. The pony's tongue felt smooth as velvet on her hand.

After lunch, Lulu took the annoying burrs out of the pony's mane. She kept the pony still by singing. "Most ponies would have to be tied for this job," she told the pony. "But you're so smart and sweet that you're staying still."

By the time Lulu picked out the last burr, she'd sung every song she knew the words to, including a few Christmas songs. The pony seemed to like "Jingle Bells" best.

That night, while brushing her teeth, Lulu looked out the bathroom window at the yards below. Wiggins was lit by the white glow of a full moon. From this second-story window Lulu had a bird's-eye view of Acorn's paddock. She could see that the Harleys had added an extension to the paddock fence. And there was Acorn looking up at it. He shook his mane, stomped his hooves, and snorted as if to say, "How could you guys ruin all my fun? I'll find another way out of this paddock. You wait and see."

Lulu heard the Harleys' back door close. She watched Anna, again in her long pink nightgown, run around the vegetable garden and through the gate into Acorn's paddock.

The little pony gaily ran over to her. After Anna gave Acorn a treat, she put her arms around his neck and hugged him.

Lulu's heart skipped a beat. "Anna and Acorn," she said wistfully to herself, "how I wish you were my friends."

The next morning Lulu went into the beauty parlor. "Grandma," she said, "I'm going for another hike. Okay?"

"Don't forget your hair appointment with

me at four o'clock," Grandmother reminded her.

"Four o'clock," Lulu echoed. She noticed a wide, flat hairbrush lying on the counter. "This is a nice brush," she said as she rubbed the stiff bristles over the palm of her hand.

"If you like it you can have it," Grandmother said. "Getting free beauty products is one of the advantages of having a grandmother who's a hairdresser."

Lulu wrapped her arms around Grandmother's waist and gave her a big hug. "Thanks, Grandma," she said. "Thank you so much."

Lulu put the brush in her backpack. Today, she thought, I'm going to brush that pony's coat until it shines.

It was another sunny day, but a little cooler than the day before. Lulu was glad that she had put a sweatshirt on over her T-shirt.

She jogged along Mudge Road. As she turned onto Lilac Lane and passed the first farm, her heart started pounding with excitement. She couldn't wait to see the white pony.

But when Lulu turned the corner in the road she didn't see the pony. She walked up to the fence. Still no pony. Had the owner taken the pony for a ride? Or had the pony only been visiting for the day? Her heart sank.

As Lulu turned to walk away, she heard a desperate, weak whinny. Looking toward the sound, she saw the white pony half hidden by a bush. The pony was lying in a far corner of the paddock and struggling to get up. Something was terribly wrong. The pony was in trouble.

A Dangerous Trap

Lulu tossed her backpack into the paddock, crawled under the fence and ran to
the pony.

As she got closer she saw that the pony's
white coat was covered with red cuts. Then
she noticed a large bloody wound on the
pony's front left leg. Lulu saw that a strand
of rusty barbed wire was wrapped around
the leg. One end of the wire was still attached to the post. The pony was trapped.

Lulu could see that the pony had gotten
jabbed by the barbs. But even worse, each

time the pony pulled to free herself, the wire around her leg would tighten and cut deeper into the flesh.

I don't care if I get cut, too, Lulu thought. I'm going to free this pony. But what could she do? One end of the barbed wire was stapled securely to the fence post. The rest was embedded in the pony's flesh. She knew she shouldn't try to untangle the pony. Not without help.

Lulu figured out that she needed a pair of wire clippers. And the pony needed a veterinarian.

The pony started to struggle again. Lulu said, "Easy, pony. Easy. That's a good pony." With Lulu's encouragement, the pony calmed down and stopped trying to get up.

Lulu realized that if she went for help, the pony would start moving again. Then that piece of rusty wire would cut deeper into the wounded leg. She decided to stay with the pony and wait for help to come to them.

She rubbed the pony's neck. Yesterday the pony's brown eyes had glowed with merriment. Today they were wide with pain and fear. They seemed to be saying, "I'm in pain and I'm afraid. Please help me."

To keep the pony calm, Lulu sang the way she had the day before.

When she saw how much the pony was sweating she fed it half of her water. Though Lulu was thirsty, too, she took only the tiniest sip to keep her voice going. She saved the rest for the pony.

Flies were buzzing around the wounds and landing on the pony. "Shoo, flies," Lulu said. She took out her map and used it to fan them away.

The sun moved across the sky.

Clip-clop. Clip-clop. Lulu heard the sound of horses' hooves on the dirt road. In the distance, she saw two people on horses. She pulled off her sweatshirt. As she waved it over her head she saw that the riders were Anna and Pam. And the two horses were their ponies — Acorn and Lightning. Lulu continued to wave her sweatshirt flag. She thought, I don't care if they think I was weird to follow Anna and Acorn yesterday. I have to get them to help this pony.

Pam yelled to Anna, "Hey, someone's signaling for help. Look."

"It's that girl from yesterday," Anna shouted.

Startled by the voices, the wounded pony began to struggle again. "Oh, pony, please don't move," Lulu said. "Everything's going to be all right."

Hearing Lulu's voice again, the pony calmed down. With one hand Lulu rubbed the pony's neck to keep her from moving. With the other hand she signaled the approaching riders to be quiet. The girls must have noticed Lulu's *shush* signal because they stopped shouting.

While Anna stayed with their ponies, Pam crawled through the fence and walked silently across the field toward Lulu and the white pony.

Lulu continued talking to the pony in a calm voice. "Pony, someone's coming to help you. If Pam can hear what I'm saying she shouldn't come any closer."

Pam stopped where she was.

Lulu continued, "Pam sees that you are caught in a piece of nasty barbed wire. We don't want to startle you because when you move the wire hurts you more. I hope she can find some wire clippers so we can cut the barbed wire. Also, she should get a vet to come as quickly as possible. I'll stay here with you, pony, until help comes."

Pam nodded solemnly at Lulu to let her know that she understood. Without a word she turned and walked out of the field. Lulu could see her talking quietly with Anna. Then the girls mounted their ponies and rode off.

Since help was on the way, Lulu decided to give the pony the rest of her water. As the pony lapped the water from her hands "Everything's going to be all right," Lulu said.

It wasn't long before Lulu saw a truck with a horse trailer bumping along the road. Pam, Anna, and a man got out of the car. Lulu was glad to see that the man was carrying a medical bag. The girls stayed at the fence while the man crawled under the fence and walked across the paddock. Lulu was glad that Anna and Pam understood that the pony might be more frightened by having a lot of people standing around.

When the man reached Lulu he whispered, "I'm Dr. Crandal, Pam's father."

Lulu said, "I'm Lulu Sanders."

Then Dr. Crandal spoke to the pony as calmly and kindly as Lulu had. "Well, pony," he said, "what kind of trouble have you gotten yourself into?"

"It's not the pony's fault," Lulu said. "The barbed-wire fence was broken."

"So I see," Dr. Crandal said. "This pony is badly hurt." While he cut the end of the wire that was still attached to the fence, the doctor asked Lulu, "Is this your pony?"

"No," Lulu said, "I was just visiting her."

All the time the doctor treated the pony, Lulu continued stroking her neck and humming softly to keep the wounded pony still.

"Well," Dr. Crandal said, "this animal certainly trusts you. Why don't you keep doing what you're doing while I administer first aid. Just move over so you can jump out of the way if she kicks."

Dr. Crandal gave the pony two shots. "One's a painkiller," he explained to Lulu. "The other is to anesthetize the area of the wound."

When he was sure the pony wouldn't feel any pain, the doctor used a pair of medical pliers to unwrap the barbed wire encircling the leg.

Then he poured antiseptic on the wound and wrapped the leg below the knee with a thick gauze bandage.

Last, he put antiseptic on the smaller cuts. "Most of these cuts need stitches," he said. "But I'm more concerned about this leg."

He looked toward the small stable that

stood in the corner of the field closest to the yellow house. "Let's get Pam and Anna over here," he said, "and see if we can't get our patient on her feet and into her stable."

After Lulu introduced herself to Anna and Pam, she explained that she was living with her grandmother. Then she said, "Pam, thank you for getting the doctor. I mean your father. I mean your father the doctor."

Pam smiled at Lulu. "I'm glad Anna and I came this way today," she said.

Dr. Crandal pulled a halter and lead rope from his medical bag. "Put this halter on the pony, Lulu," he said. "Let's see if she can stand up."

As Lulu gently placed the halter over the pony's pink nose, she tried not to think of what would happen if the pony couldn't stand. She knew that horses with broken legs were shot.

"Okay, Lulu, ask her to get up," Dr. Crandal said.

Lulu stood in front of the pony, saying,

"Come on, pony. Stand up. You can do it."

The pony tried. And tried. On the third try, teetering and tottering, she struggled awkwardly to her feet. Anna, Pam, and Lulu exchanged happy smiles. But Dr. Crandal remained serious. "Let's see if she'll walk," he said.

"Come on, pony," Lulu said. She looked back over her shoulder. The pony moved in a slow unsteady gait, putting almost no weight on the wounded leg.

Pam and Anna ran ahead to check out the stable. Lulu and the doctor moved across the field at the pony's slow, crippled pace. When they finally got the pony to the stable, Pam and Anna met them at the door.

"We changed the straw. What a mess," Pam said.

"The water bucket was filthy," Anna said. "We had to wash it out before we put in the fresh water."

Pam told her father, "I think this pony's

been neglected. You should say something to her owner."

"I've got more important things to talk to the owner about," Dr. Crandal said. He explained that the pony needed more than the emergency care he'd given her. "But I can't do X rays and treat her," he said, "before I talk to the owner."

"You keep saying, 'the owner,' Dad," Pam said. "Don't you know who it is?"

"I've never treated this pony," he said. "Some new folks moved into this place a while back. I've been trying to remember their names."

"It says 'Baxter' on the mailbox," Pam said.

"Good for you, honey," Dr. Crandal said. "That's it. I've noticed this pony when I've driven by. I figured I'd hear from the Baxters sooner or later." He gave the pony a kindly pat. "Poor animal, I didn't expect to meet you this way."

The three girls remained silent as Dr.

Crandal thought about what to do. "I remember hearing that the Baxters are in real estate. They bought Ritter Real Estate. You girls stay with the pony while I take a run over there."

Lulu followed Dr. Crandal out of the stable. "Dr. Crandal," she asked, "if the Baxters don't want to spend the money to have their pony treated, could they just, you know . . ." She couldn't finish the question.

Dr. Crandal finished it for her. "Have it put to sleep?"

She nodded.

"I know that sounds terrible to you, Lulu, but the pony belongs to its owners. It's their property. So it's their decision whether the pony receives treatment."

Lulu nodded again. She felt Dr. Crandal's hand on her shoulder.

He shook his head and said, "But to be honest with you, at this point I don't even know if the pony can be saved."

Lulu's Reward

When Lulu came back into the pony's stall, Anna was telling Pam, "I've got to go now. I promised my mother I'd be home by five to help her with a party at the diner."

"You're coming to my house tonight, right?" Pam asked.

"Yes, my mom said she'd drop me off," Anna said. "Are you sure it's okay for Acorn to stay, too?"

"Sure," Pam answered.

Lulu looked at her watch. It was already four-thirty. "Anna, when you get home could you tell my grandmother why I'm not home?"

"Sure," Anna said. She frowned. "Your grandmother really doesn't like ponies, does she?"

"I guess not," Lulu mumbled. "She's not much of an outdoor person."

"But you like ponies," Anna said.

"I love them," Lulu said. She combed her fingers through the injured pony's mane. "Especially this one."

"I hope the pony is okay," Anna said as she left the stable.

A few minutes later, Pam pointed over the wall separating the pony's stall from the storage area. "Look Lulu," she said excitedly. "There are a bunch of award ribbons."

Lulu scratched the pony's forelock, "Good for you, pony," she said. "You're a winner."

Pam went into the storage area and climbed on a bale of hay to get a closer look at the ribbons. "Wow," she exclaimed. "Lots

of them are first place. And there's a blanket in here with her name on it."

"What is it?" Lulu asked.

" 'Snow White,' " Pam read.

At the sound of her name Snow White turned her head toward Pam and whinnied, as if to say, "That's it. That's my name."

"Snow White," Lulu repeated. She looked into the pony's eyes. "What a perfect name for you. Well, Snow White, it's a pleasure to meet you." Lulu could tell by the look in Snow White's eyes that she liked hearing her name.

When Pam came back to the stall side of the stable, Lulu asked her, "Do you see a lot of injured horses at your father's animal clinic?"

"All the time," Pam said. "I help out. Especially when we have injured animals boarding in our stables."

There was a moment of silence.

"Do you think Snow White will get better?" Lulu asked.

Pam said yes and tried to smile, but Lulu saw tears in her eys. Pam turned from Lulu and walked to the doorway. "I'll stand here," she said, "so I can see if the Baxters come."

While they waited, Pam asked Lulu questions about where she came from and why she was in Wiggins. She wanted to know all about her riding lessons in England.

Lulu learned some things about Pam, too. She found out that her brother and sister were five-year-old twins named Jack and Jill. And that she had had her own ponies since she was five. Lightning was her second pony.

Both girls heard the car coming down the dirt road. "The car turned into the driveway," Pam said. "It must be Mr. Baxter. I'll go tell him what happened."

"Don't forget the part about how brave and wonderful Snow White has been," Lulu said.

"I'm also going to tell him how great you've been," Pam said. "You're a hero. You should have a reward."

While Pam was gone, Lulu daydreamed that Snow White would be cured of all her injuries. And that the owner would be so grateful that he would give her Snow White as a reward. She was imagining her first ride on Snow White when her daydream was interrupted by a harsh, angry voice.

"What have you done to my daughter's pony?" a man's voice bellowed. A big bulk of a man stood in the stable doorway.

Snow White snorted.

Lulu stood up and said, "Nothing. She was caught in barbed wire. I waited for help."

Just then Dr. Crandal walked into the stable. Lulu sighed with relief. Maybe he could get this horrid man to stop yelling. He was upsetting Snow White.

Dr. Crandal introduced himself.

"I'm Brook Baxter. What's going on here?" the man said.

Dr. Crandal explained that the pony's leg was seriously injured. "I won't know if it can be treated until I've taken X rays. And even if it's a wound that can be stitched, we won't know for a week or so if the leg has responded to the treatment."

"If it can be treated and she recovers, what kind of shape is she going to be in?" Mr. Baxter asked.

"I can't tell you if she'll completely recover the use of that leg," Dr. Crandal answered, "anymore than I can predict if I can save your pony. The tendon — "

Mr. Baxter interrupted Dr. Crandal. "What you're saying is I could spend a lot of money on an animal that could be useless or have to be put down."

"Yes," Dr. Crandal said. "That's what I'm saying."

Mr. Baxter turned to Lulu and yelled, "It's all your fault, young lady. Trespassing on private property and getting that dumb animal to run where she had no business running."

"She's not dumb," Lulu protested, "and I — "

Mr. Baxter cut off Lulu by turning to Dr. Crandal. "Just put the creature out of its misery," he said. Then he pointed at Lulu. "And I hold this girl responsible."

"Mr. Baxter, just what is it that you hold Lucinda responsible for?" a woman's voice asked.

Everyone, including Snow White, was startled by the loud voice. They all looked to the door to see Mrs. Sanders standing in the doorway.

Before Mr. Baxter could answer, Grandmother was telling Lulu, "Come to me, child." Then she ordered in her sternest voice, "All of you, come out here. I want an explanation for what is going on."

Who's Going to Pay?

Pam stayed in the stable with Snow White while Lulu, Dr. Crandal, Mr. Baxter, and Grandmother Sanders gathered outside. Even though Lulu was dirty, Grandmother put a protective arm around her shoulder.

Mr. Baxter and Grandmother glared at one another. "Do I know you?" he asked.

"I know you," she answered. "I'm your wife's new hairdresser. I did your daughter Rema's hair, too. How dare you take that tone with my grandchild? Now what is going on here? You'd better be straight with me."

Lulu was amazed that Grandmother was taking her side without even asking her what happened.

When Mr. Baxter began his accusation that Lulu had trespassed on his property and that it was her fault that the pony was injured, Dr. Crandal interrupted.

"Mrs. Sanders," Dr. Crandal said, "your granddaughter did the right thing. She found a pony in trouble and she stayed with the animal until someone came along to help." The doctor turned to Mr. Baxter, "You should be thanking Lulu, Mr. Baxter, not accusing her."

"Thank her for what?" Mr. Baxter said. "That my pony has to be put down?"

Lulu spoke up. "But Snow White doesn't have to be put down. I'll pay for the medical bills. I have a bank account."

"Lucinda," Grandmother said, "that's your allowance for the year."

"Everyone calm down," Dr. Crandal said.

"Snow White is Mr. Baxter's pony. The medical bills will be sent to him."

Having her grandmother's arm around her shoulder gave Lulu courage. "What about your daughter?" she asked. "She must love her pony."

"Rema's in boarding school. I wanted to sell the pony before she left," Mr. Baxter snapped.

"She probably wants her pony to be here when she comes home for vacation," Lulu said.

As if to plead her own case, Snow White whinnied from the stable.

Mr. Baxter fell silent for a second. Then he turned all his attention to Lulu. "I'll tell you what," he said. "I'll pay the medical bills. But if she has to be put down, you'll pay me back for my expenses."

"It's a deal," Lulu said. She extended her hand to shake on it. Mr. Baxter didn't move. "I said it's a deal," Lulu repeated. Mr. Baxter finally shook her hand.

"So it's settled," Dr. Crandal said. "Let's

get Snow White over to my animal clinic. We've wasted enough time."

Mr. Baxter looked at his watch. "I'm late for an appointment to show a property. Call me tonight, Dr. Crandal, and let me know what's up." He turned and stomped out of the stable.

"Come along now, Lucinda," Grandmother said.

Lulu looked up into her grandmother's stern face and asked, "Please, can I lead Snow White into the trailer? She might be scared."

Grandmother sighed. "I'll wait in the car. But be quick. We have bingo tonight." Lulu knew better than to ask her grandmother if she could go with Snow White to the animal clinic.

Once Snow White was safely inside the trailer, Lulu put her cheek against her neck. "Bye, Snow White," she whispered. "Good luck."

"I'll call you as soon as my dad tells me

how Snow White is doing, okay?" Pam said.

"Okay," Lulu said. "Thanks."

As Grandmother and Lulu drove down Lilac Lane behind the trailer, tears came rolling down Lulu's cheeks. "Snow White might die," she said. "Maybe her leg can't be fixed."

"You'll just have to wait and see, Lucinda," Grandmother said. "You've done everything you could."

Lulu remembered something that she should tell her grandmother right away. "Thank you, Grandma," she said, "for defending me with Mr. Baxter. I know you don't like horses."

"I may not like horses, my dear," Grandmother said, "but I think a great deal of you. It was clear that you had put yourself out to help a living creature. What you did for that horse was just the sort of thing your father would have done. Your mother, too, for that matter. I'm proud of you."

Now Grandmother had tears in her eyes, too.

But by the time Lulu and Grandmother got back to the house on Main Street, Grandmother was back to being her old fussy self. "Now take off those filthy shoes and clothes, Lucinda, before you step on the carpet. Bring them right down to the laundry room, sneakers and all. And for goodness sakes, take a shower and wash that hair. And put on a dress."

Half an hour later Lulu was starting down the back stairs, clean and in her good dress. The phone rang. Lulu ran down the stairs into the kitchen. But Grandmother had already answered the phone and was saying, "Well, thank you so much, Mrs. Crandal. It's very thoughtful of you. But Lucinda is going to bingo tonight. Perhaps she could come for a sleepover another time."

Lulu fell to her knees at Grandmother's feet and clasped her hands in a begging position.

Grandmother looked at her in horror and signaled her to get up. While Grandmother chatted on with Mrs. Crandal about what a huge success the bingo games had been as a church fund-raiser, Lulu scribbled a note.

It's hard to make friends in a new place. Please, please can I go? Pam's a very nice girl.

She put the note in front of Grandmother. Grandmother read it, then studied Lulu with a level serious gaze and told Mrs. Crandal that Lulu could go to the sleepover.

After Grandmother hung up, Lulu showered her with kisses and thank-yous.

"Well, good gracious, child," Grandmother said.

As Lulu was changing back into jeans and packing her overnight bag, she wasn't only thinking about her new friend, Pam. She was thinking about her new pony friend, Snow White.

Half an hour later the Crandals picked

up Lulu. Mrs. Crandal was driving. Pam and the twins sat in the backseats. Lulu got in next to Pam. Before she could ask, Pam said, "My father's still working on Snow White. We don't know any more about her condition."

Lulu held back from asking if she'd be able to visit Snow White in the animal clinic.

The Crandals' house was spacious and comfortable. Lulu especially liked the large kitchen with a big couch in the corner and a round oak table in the middle of the room.

Mrs. Crandal went right to the stove to finish cooking dinner. Lulu and Pam set the table.

A few minutes later Lulu faced a plate heaped high with steaming spaghetti. Just as she was about to lift a big forkful to her mouth, Dr. Crandal came in.

Lulu's heart started to pound. Her hunger disappeared. She put her fork down.

"Well," Dr. Crandal said. "Glad to see you here, Lulu. It'll save me a phone call."

"How's Snow White?" Lulu managed to ask.

"I was able to stitch her up," he said. "If the barbed wire had dug in another quarter of an inch I wouldn't have been able to repair the leg. Your keeping her still the way you did saved her life."

Everyone at the table clapped.

When they'd quieted down, Lulu asked Dr. Crandal, "Will she be able to carry a rider and jump again?"

"We won't know that for a couple of weeks," Dr. Crandal answered. "It depends on how well she recovers. She'll need a lot of care."

"We'll take care of her," Pam said. She looked at Lulu, "Won't we?"

"Yes," Lulu said. "Yes, we will." She stood up. "Could I go see her right now?"

"Sit down and eat your dinner and let the pony rest. She's all drugged-up right now anyway," Dr. Crandal said.

Lulu sat back down. Pam leaned over and whispered in her ear. "When I invited you to a sleepover, I didn't say where we were going to sleep."

"Where?" Lulu whispered back.

Pam whispered to Lulu, "In the barn. With Snow White."

Lulu had no trouble having two big helpings of spaghetti and a bunch of the best chocolate cookies she'd ever eaten.

Snow White's Sleepover

After they did the dishes, Lulu and Pam headed out to the barn with their sleeping bags. The full harvest moon glowed on the horizon.

"Look, the moon is so bright you can see the yellow and orange leaves on the sugar maple tree," Pam said.

Lulu liked that Pam noticed things like that. "That's just the sort of thing my dad says," Lulu giggled.

The girls passed the horse paddock.

Acorn's and Lightning's coats were glowing in the moonlight.

When they got to the barn, Lulu asked, "Which stall is Snow White in?"

"The last on the right," Pam answered.

Lulu was suddenly very anxious to be with Snow White. She dropped her sleeping bag and ran through the barn until she came to the last stall. Looking over the wooden gate, she saw Snow White standing in the corner. Her injured leg was wrapped in a huge bandage. Lulu also noticed little stitches dotting the pony's white coat like stiff black hairs. She felt sad for all that the pony had been through.

She went into the stall. "Hi, Snow White," she said quietly. "How are you feeling?"

Snow White didn't even look up.

Pam came in behind Lulu and said, "She must be very tired from everything."

"Look at all the stitches," Lulu whispered. "And her leg. How can she walk with that thing? It goes up over her hock. She can't bend her leg."

"That's the idea," Pam explained. "My dad says that the bandage is supposed to keep her leg stiff so the stitches will stay in place and the wound will heal." Then Pam went back outside to feed Acorn and Lightning.

While she was gone, Dr. Crandal came in to tell Lulu what to do for Snow White that night.

"We'll know that Snow White is on the road to recovery," Dr. Crandal concluded, "when she's eating and moving around."

When Dr. Crandal left, Lulu made a neat copy of his instructions.

To take care of Snow White tonight
1. Give plenty of water
2. Try to get S.W. to eat hay
3. Try to get S.W. to walk
4. Call doctor (on barn phone) if any questions or problems

Pam came back into the barn with Anna, who had arrived for the sleepover. While Snow White slept, the girls set up the empty stall next to Snow White's with their sleeping bags. Anna patted her backpack and said, "I brought over some quiches and kiwi tarts left over from the party my mother catered."

"Sometimes," Pam told Lulu, "Anna brings the weirdest things to school for lunch."

At the mention of school, they all said together, "What grade are you in?" Pam and Anna were asking Lulu. And Lulu was asking them.

They answered in unison, too. "Fifth grade."

All three girls laughed and hit high fives.

"How many fifth-grade classes are there?" Lulu asked.

"Only one," Anna said.

"So," Pam said, "we're all in the same class."

"And," Anna continued, "our teacher,

Mr. Livingston, is nice. You'll like him."

The girls yelled "All right!" and hit high fives again. They were all giggling. But not so loudly that they didn't hear Snow White neigh.

"She's awake!" Lulu shouted.

They ran to the pony's stall. Snow White was finally awake, but still standing in the corner. Lulu motioned the other two girls to stand back while she went up to the pony.

"It's all right, Snow White," Lulu said. "You're going to be okay. You probably feel a little drowsy from the medicine Dr. Crandal gave you. But you're going to be fine."

Snow White neighed again.

Lulu offered the pony water, but Snow White refused. Remembering their time together in the field, Lulu dipped into the pail and offered Snow White a slosh of water in her cupped hand. Snow White lapped the water. After that the pony drank more water from the pail.

"It would be a good sign," Lulu said, "if she'd eat and move around."

"Maybe it would work better if Lulu were alone with her," Anna suggested.

Pam agreed and the two girls started to leave the stall. Snow White snorted.

The three girls laughed.

Snow White whinnied and nodded her head, as if to say, "I want you all to stay."

"I think she likes the sound of our voices," Lulu said.

So for the next hour Pam, Anna, and Lulu visited with Snow White. The girls had so much to learn about one another that there wasn't a moment of silence.

Around ten o'clock Pam said they should go outside and check on Acorn and Lightning. "I'll stay here. I want to get Snow White to eat. And walk a little, too," Lulu said.

"I think we're babying her too much," Pam said. "If we leave her alone I bet she'll try to do more."

Anna took Lulu's hand and gave her a little pull. "Come on."

Lulu hated to leave Snow White, even for a little while. But if it meant that the pony might walk, she would go.

After the girls checked on Lightning and Acorn, they returned to the barn. Lulu was the first to see Snow White's head sticking out over the stall door.

"Snow White!" Lulu shouted as she ran toward the pony. "You walked!"

Snow White snorted at her, as if to say, "Where were you?"

Lulu stroked the pony's muzzle and said, "Good for you, Snow White."

A few minutes later Snow White was munching on hay.

Then Lulu got her to walk a few more steps. "I wonder if the stiff leg hurts when she walks?" Lulu asked.

"Probably," a man's voice answered. The girls and Snow White all turned to see Dr. Crandal standing at the stall door. He was smiling at them. "But with you three to distract her, she can't be feeling too badly."

Dr. Crandal was very impressed with the pony's progress. "This is a terrific pony," he said. "Somewhere along the line she's had good care and a lot of human company. She loves people."

"I guess it was that girl Rema," Lulu said.

"But her father doesn't care about Snow White one bit and he was so mean to Lulu, Dad."

"I just talked to Mr. Baxter," Dr. Crandal said. "He's been under a lot of stress with his new business. Also his wife's been in California because her father's in the hospital."

"That's no excuse for not trying to save an animal who's been hurt," Lulu said.

"Well," Dr. Crandal said, "with you girls taking care of her, this pony has a good chance for recovery."

Dr. Crandal told the girls they should let Snow White rest and get some sleep themselves.

Anna and Pam said good night to the pony. Lulu waited until Snow White was fast asleep before joining them in the stall they'd set up for their sleepover.

She found Anna and Pam still wide-awake and talking.

"Wouldn't it be wonderful," Anna said to Lulu, "if Snow White were your pony? Then we'd all have ponies."

Lulu got into her sleeping bag. "For now," she said, "let's pretend Snow White *is* my pony."

They all agreed and lay awake talking about all the things they'd do together on their ponies. It was a long list.

The Best Medicine

Anna and Pam were right about the fifth-grade class at Wiggins Elementary. The teacher — Mr. Livingston — was nice, and the other kids in the fifth grade were okay, too. But Lulu Sanders had only one thing on her mind during her first week at Wiggins Elementary. Snow White.

Every morning that week she got up at six o'clock. By six-thirty she was out of the house and riding an old bike she'd borrowed from Anna's older sister. She'd pedal through the chilly early morning mist to the Crandals' barn.

Lulu would run into the barn calling, "Morning, Snow White." The pony would show how happy she was to see Lulu by putting her head over the stall door and whinnying. After giving Snow White a fresh pail of water to drink, Lulu would muck out the pony's stall. Using a pitchfork, she removed the manure and the wet straw and put them in a wheelbarrow. Then she stacked the straw that wasn't soiled in a corner so she could sweep the floor.

Lulu would then add pitchforks of fresh, dry straw to the stall. She wanted Snow White to have an extra comfortable stall while her leg was healing.

Next, Lulu crushed up Snow White's pills and put them in her oats. She had to see that the pony ate all the oats so she'd get all the medicine.

While Lulu was taking care of Snow

White, Pam was also in the barn doing her morning chores.

Lulu's last two chores were to make sure there was hay and fresh water for Snow White to have during the day.

When Pam and Lulu finished in the barn, they washed up in the tack room and rode bikes together to school.

During the day, Dr. Crandal checked on Snow White. He'd take off the big bandage, see how the wound was healing, change the dressing, and put the bandage back on.

After school each day Lulu did everything for Snow White that she'd done in the morning — all over again. But in the afternoon she also had time to groom Snow White and hand-walk her in the barn. Every day Snow White walked a little farther down the aisle between the stalls.

Lulu made a chart to keep track of the chores she had to do for Snow White.

Friday afternoon, as Lulu and Pam

		Tues.	Wed.	Thurs.	Fri.
Muck out stall	A.M.	✓	✓	✓	✓
	P.M.	✓	✓	✓	
Lay in two sections of fresh hay	A.M.	✓	✓	✓	✓
	P.M.	✓	✓	✓	
Clean and refill water buckets	A.M.	✓	✓	✓	✓
	P.M.	✓	✓	✓	
Two handfuls of oats with pills	A.M.	✓	✓	✓	✓
	P.M.	✓	✓	✓	
Grooming	P.M.	✓	✓	✓	
Hand walk		2 min.	4 min.	6 min.	
Check leg and change dressing shot		✓	✓	✓	

turned their bikes onto Riddle Road, Lulu screamed. "Snow White's outside! Look, Pam."

They pumped hard on their bikes to get to the paddock as fast as they could. Pam's mother was leading Snow White slowly toward them. The twins sat on the paddock fence cheering Snow White on.

73

"Snow White!" Lulu shouted as she climbed over the fence and ran up to the pony.

Snow White nuzzled Lulu.

"Dr. Crandal is so impressed with her progress that we thought she should get some fresh air and a little walk today," Mrs. Crandal said as she smiled at Lulu. "I also thought it would be a nice surprise for you." She handed Lulu the lead rope and gave her a hug around the shoulders. "You've given Snow White the best medicine in the world, Lulu. T.L.C. Do you know what T.L.C. stands for?"

"Tender Loving Care," Lulu said.

Mrs. Crandal nodded. "That's right. Dr. Crandal says he's never seen a leg wound heal up so fast. You've done a super job of nursing, Lulu. Snow White's about ready to go home."

Lulu suddenly felt all the happiness drain out of her. "Go home?" she whispered. "You mean back to Mr. Baxter?"

"Snow White is his pony," Mrs. Crandal

said. "I'm sure he'll let you visit her. After all, you saved her life."

"He probably wishes Snow White died," Pam said, "so Lulu would have to pay and he wouldn't have to spend all his money."

"Now Pam," Mrs. Crandal said, "be fair. According to your father, Mr. Baxter's been under a lot of pressure lately."

Lulu could hear Pam and her mother talking, but she wasn't paying any attention to what they said. She was looking into Snow White's eyes. "I'll still take care of you, Snow White," she whispered. "I promise. I'll find a way."

"Acorn! Acorn!" Jack and Jill were shouting. Lulu saw that Anna and her Shetland pony were coming off Pony Pal Trail. The twins raced one another to open the paddock gate. Lightning whinnied as she ran along the fence of the side paddock. She was greeting Acorn, too.

Snow White snorted, but not happily. "It's okay, Snow White," Lulu said. "Lightning and Acorn are your pals."

Mrs. Crandal said Anna should put Acorn in the side paddock with Lightning. "Until they get used to Snow White and she gets used to them," she said. "Especially since Snow White has an injury."

Mrs. Crandal went back to the animal clinic to finish her day's work. The twins joined Lightning and Acorn in the side paddock. And the three friends sat in a row on the paddock fence near Snow White.

"This is the first time our ponies are together," Anna said. "Even though they're in different paddocks you can see them all at once. Three ponies. Three girls. Six Pony Pals."

"Five Pony Pals," Lulu said. "I can't pretend that Snow White is mine anymore. She's going back to the Baxters."

Pam jumped off the fence and shouted, "It isn't fair." She put her hands on her hips and faced Anna and Lulu. "Mr. Baxter doesn't want a pony and doesn't have time to take care of her. Lulu wants a pony and

does have the time to take care of her. The fair thing is that Lulu should have the pony."

"Especially because she saved Snow White's life," Anna said.

"You're both acting like Snow White is Mr. Baxter's pony," Lulu said. "But really she is Rema's pony."

A car pulled into the driveway. Lulu figured it was someone going to the animal clinic, but Pam recognized the car. "He's here," she said.

"Who?" Lulu and Anna asked.

"Mr. Baxter," Pam answered. "And there's someone with him."

Lulu jumped down from the fence and stood next to Snow White like she was the pony's bodyguard. She watched Mr. Baxter and a woman get out of the car.

As soon as the woman saw Snow White she ran ahead of Mr. Baxter calling, "Snow White. Oh poor Snow White."

Snow White turned toward the voice and

whinnied. Lulu knew by the happy sound in the whinny and the curl of the pony's lips that Snow White liked the woman.

"Are you the girl who saved Snow White's life?" the woman asked.

"Yes," Lulu said.

The woman had tears in her eyes. "I'm Mrs. Baxter," she said. "We're all so grateful. Rema's been worried sick about Snow White. We've all been so worried."

Lulu noticed that Mr. Baxter didn't even say hello to Snow White. He just looked at the big bandage and shook his head in disgust.

Mrs. Crandal joined the group at the paddock fence. After she introduced herself, she explained to the Baxters that Snow White could go home. She told them, "In another week the bandage will be removed. But you must understand that it will be months before she's as strong and limber as she was before the accident."

Lulu noticed that Mr. Baxter's face got

that angry look again. "So, she still needs a lot of care," he said.

Mrs. Crandal agreed. "The vet should check her every day until the bandage is off. After that she'll need leg soaks. And, of course, regular exercise."

Mrs. Baxter turned to her husband. "We're at work all day. And the fence needs to be replaced."

"Maybe you should leave Snow White here," Pam said.

Mr. Baxter shook his head. "Boarding an animal is expensive."

"Lulu's been taking care of Snow White for free," Mrs. Crandal explained. "And doing a wonderful job. We're only charging you for medical care and food."

"I love ponies and I know a lot about them from when I lived in England," Lulu said. She stroked Snow White's neck. Snow White lovingly nuzzled Lulu's shoulder.

"Lulu knows as much about ponies as I do and I grew up with them," Pam said.

The Baxters looked at one another and nodded in agreement. "We'll leave Snow White here for another three weeks," Mrs. Baxter said.

The Pony Pals cheered — and hugged Snow White.

9

Whose Pony Is It?

After the Baxters left, Lulu led Snow White back to her stall. As she rubbed her down she told her, "Snow White, you're my pony for another three weeks."

"We've got to do better than that," Pam said. Lulu looked up to see her two friends leaning on the stall gate.

"We should think real hard about how Snow White can be Lulu's pony," Anna said.

"We would have so much fun if you had a pony too, Lulu," Pam said.

Lulu pictured them all riding on Pony Pal Trail. Anna was on her feisty Shetland, the little brown Acorn. Pam was on her sleek Connemara, the red Lightning. And she was on the sweetest Welsh pony in the world, Snow White. Lulu couldn't think of anything that would make her happier.

"My mother invited both you guys to dinner," Pam said.

"I can't," Lulu said. "My grandmother's doing my hair tonight. I can't put it off any longer."

Anna imitated Lulu's grandmother. "Oh, Lucinda dear, we must do something with that hair. I think a lovely purple color and a few million curls would be nice."

They all giggled. "Okay, you guys," Lulu said. "Just promise you won't laugh when you see me tomorrow."

Pam turned very serious. "Tomorrow," she said, "we should each have a plan for how we can get Snow White for Lulu. For keeps. Write out your idea."

*　　*　　*

Two hours later Grandmother was combing out Lulu's freshly washed hair. Lulu could see Grandmother's stern expression in the mirror when she asked Lulu, "How much longer will you be taking care of the Baxter girl's horse?"

"Just another couple of weeks," Lulu said.

"I don't like it," Grandmother scolded. "The Baxters should be taking care of their own animal." Grandmother picked up the scissors and began cutting.

"When you cut Rema Baxter's hair, what was she like?" Lulu asked.

"Let me see," Grandmother answered. "Her hair's a beautiful dark brown. Nice and thick."

Lulu interrupted. "I meant what's *she* like. Was she nice? Or did she act like a snob?"

"Rema Baxter was very mannerly," Grandmother said. "She seemed excited about going away to boarding school. She said Wiggins was too small for her. She's attending an excellent school."

Lulu turned toward her grandmother and asked excitedly, "Do you know the name and everything?" she said.

"My dear!" Grandmother said with alarm. "Do stay still. I almost cut your earlobe just then."

"Sorry," Lulu said. She turned back to the mirror and talked to her grandmother's reflection. "What's the name of Rema's school, Grandma?"

"She attends Clinton Hall," Grandmother said. "A private girls' academy in Delaware."

Clinton Hall in Delaware. Lulu repeated it to herself so she wouldn't forget.

The next morning the Pony Pals met at the Crandals'. Since Acorn and Lightning were grazing in the main paddock, Lulu put Snow White in the side one. Anna and Pam were sitting on the grass with their backs against the fence waiting for her. As Lulu came toward her friends, Anna called, "Your hair looks great."

"No purple," Lulu said.

"And no fake curls," Pam added.

The Pony Pals laughed.

"Okay, everyone, take out your plans for getting Snow White for Lulu," Pam said.

Lulu noticed that Snow White was cautiously making her way toward the fence that divided her from Lightning and Acorn.

Lulu said, "Let's hear yours first, Pam."

Pam unfolded a piece of paper and read.

Lulu buys Snow White with her allowance money.

"It's a perfect idea," Pam said. "Didn't Mr. Baxter say he wished he'd sold Snow White already?"

"He didn't sell her because of Rema, remember?" Lulu said. "And Mrs. Baxter seems to really like Snow White, too."

"If Lulu spends all her money buying Snow White, how can she pay to keep her?" Anna asked. "Don't forget that it costs money to feed a pony, especially in the winter."

"Plus," Lulu said, "my father's project in the Amazon ends in June. I'll be leaving Wiggins."

"I didn't know that," Pam said.

"Me either," Anna said.

Both girls looked very sad.

Lulu liked her new friends so much that she felt sad herself. She asked, "So, what's your idea, Anna?"

Anna unfolded a piece of drawing paper. "I drew mine," she said.

"My idea," Anna explained, "is that Lulu should rent Snow White from the Baxters. That's not as expensive as buying her.

We're leasing Acorn. Lots of people lease ponies. And Snow White can live with Acorn in his paddock. My parents said it'd be okay. There's plenty of room in the pony shelter, too."

"What a great idea," Pam said. "That way Acorn will have a stablemate. My dad said that Acorn's always trying to get out of his paddock because he's lonely."

"So it would be good for Acorn and it would be good for Snow White," Anna said.

"And it'd be perfect for Rema," Lulu added. "She comes home for the summer just about the same time as I'm leaving." Lulu didn't let herself think too much about how sad it would be to part with Snow White in June. She needed to use all her energy to figure out how she could have her until then.

"But there's a problem," Lulu told Anna and Pam. "I'd have to buy a saddle and helmet. Bridles, too. All that tack stuff is expensive."

"Maybe you could rent Rema's tack from the Baxters," Pam said.

"Great idea," Lulu said.

"Look!" Anna was pointing toward the ponies.

The girls looked up to see that Acorn and Snow White were nose to nose at the fence separating the two paddocks. "They're getting to know one another by smelling each other's breath," Pam explained. "They'd make great stablemates."

"What was your idea?" Anna asked Lulu.

Lulu handed Anna a piece of paper. "It fits right in with your idea," she said. "Read it out loud."

Anna wouldn't take the paper. "No," she said. "It's your idea. You read it."

Lulu read:

Write a letter to Rema Baxter and ask her if I can take care of Snow White while she's at school. Also tell her that I'd like to ride Snow White.

"Perfect," Pam said. "I bet the Baxters will agree to let you take care of Snow White if Rema says it's okay. Let's write the letter right now."

"Great," Lulu said. "Then we can get the school's address from the library."

When they'd finished the letter, Pam said, "It's a good letter. We got everything in."

"I like that you signed it 'Lucinda,' " Anna said. "And used big words like, 'proper arrangements.' If she's as stuck-up as I think she is, she'll love that stuff."

"What about when she comes home for vacations?" Pam asked. "Won't she want to ride her pony?"

Lulu added a P.S. to the letter saying that during vacations, Snow White could stay at Rema's. She also reminded Rema that the paddock fence should be replaced.

"Just one more thing," Lulu told her friends. She added a P.P.S. and read it aloud. "Snow White says 'Hi.' "

"Now," Pam said, "it's a perfect letter."

10

On Pony Pal Trail

The first thing Lulu did after school every day was to flip through the pile of mail on the kitchen counter. Day after day she was disappointed. There was no mail for her. No letter from Rema.

And every day while having an afternoon snack in the beauty parlor, she'd ask her grandmother, "Did I get any calls today?"

Grandmother would say, "No, dear. Are you expecting a call?"

And Lulu would say, "Just wondered."

As the days went by, Snow White was getting stronger and stronger. And so was Lulu's love for her.

Meanwhile Lulu wasn't spending any of her allowance money. She'd figured out that leasing a pony and paying for feed would cost more than twenty-five dollars a week. This worried her. What if Rema and her parents said she could lease Snow White and she couldn't afford it?

Three weeks passed this way.

It was a Saturday afternoon. Lulu was in Acorn's stall helping Anna give him an extra-special grooming before going over to Pam's on Pony Pal Trail.

"I can't believe Rema hasn't answered my letter," Lulu said.

Anna looked up from combing out Acorn's mane. "I told you she was a snob."

"But my grandmother said Rema had good manners," Lulu said.

"With grown-ups maybe," Anna said. "But I bet she's not nice to other kids."

"You're probably right," Lulu said. "I bet she thinks I'm just this little kid who's too young to take care of her pony."

"Lucinda! Lucinda!" Grandmother was yelling to Lulu from the back steps. "Come in, dear. To the beauty parlor."

Lulu shouted "Coming!" to her grandmother. She put down the rub cloth she was using on Acorn and said, "She probably wants me to go to the store. I'll come back as fast as I can."

When Lulu came into the beauty parlor, Grandmother looked up from the head of brown hair that she was cutting. She pointed her scissors at the corner of the desk and said, "A letter came for you. From Rema Baxter. You've been so interested in the mail lately, I thought you'd want to know right away."

Lulu already had the letter in her hand. "Thanks, Grandma," she said as she ran from the beauty parlor.

Grandmother called after her, "Lucinda, no running . . ."

But Lulu was already out the door and on her way back to Anna's.

She was breathless when she got there. "I got a letter from Rema," she said. She handed Anna the letter. "You open it and read it to me. I'm too nervous."

Anna opened the letter much too slowly for Lulu's taste. Finally she pulled out the letter. And handed it to Lulu.

"It's a letter written to you," she said. "You read it."

Lulu read:

Dear Lucinda:

My parents and I have discussed your offer to lease Snow White. We propose the following business arrangement.

1. Lucinda Sanders takes care of Snow White in a paddock to be inspected by Mrs. Baxter.

2. Lucinda Sanders pays for Snow White's feed. All other expenses to be paid for by Mr. and Mrs. Baxter.

3. Lucinda Sanders will send a monthly written report on Snow White's health to me.
4. There will be no leasing fee.

If you agree to the above tell my parents.

By the way my parents are the only ones who call me "Rema." Everyone else calls me "Rae." Do you have a nickname?

Sincerely,

Rae

P.S.
I forgot to say that you can borrow my tack. But it must be maintained in good condition.
P.P.S.
Give Snow White a big hug and kiss from me.

When Lulu finished reading the letter, she and Anna hugged one another and jumped up and down. Then, suddenly, Lulu stopped and became serious.

"What's wrong?" Anna said. "It couldn't be more perfect."

"My grandmother has to agree," Lulu said. "And you know how she feels about ponies."

"Show her Rema's letter," Anna suggested. "It's a very proper letter and your grandmother likes that sort of thing."

Again Lulu ran through the paddock, over the fence, through Grandmother's yard, and into the house. She walked through the dining room and into the beauty parlor. Lulu handed her Grandmother the letter.

When she'd finished reading, Grandmother tapped the letter with a comb and said, "Lucinda, what would your father say to all this? I mean if you were able to reach him and ask his permission to have a pony."

Lulu told her grandmother, "Dad would say it was wonderful. That it was a great opportunity to have a pony without spending a lot of money. Dad would say that taking care of an animal will teach me responsibility. He'd say that I'm a good rider and I know a lot about ponies."

"Yes," Grandmother agreed, "he would say all those things." She handed the letter back to Lulu. "Well, I suppose it will be easier if the animal is right next door. I don't like you riding about on that bicycle so early in the morning."

Lulu hugged her grandmother. "Thank you. Thank you," she gushed.

A few minutes later Lulu was walking and jogging beside Anna and Acorn as they rode on Pony Pal Trail toward the Crandals'.

"I can't believe that Snow White is mine," Lulu said. "Until June anyway."

"We're going to have so much fun," Anna said. "I'm so glad it's you and Snow White and not Rema and Snow White. Don't you think she sounded snobby in that letter?"

"I thought it was the most wonderful letter in the world," Lulu said. "And her name is 'Rae.' We should call her that from now on."

They both saw Pam and Lightning coming toward them from the opposite direction on Pony Pal Trail.

"Yes! Yes! Yes!" Pam shouted. "It's the best news I've ever heard."

"I called and told Pam right away," Anna said.

"That's okay," Lulu said. "As long as I'm the one who tells Snow White."

Lulu gave Lightning a pat on the neck as she asked Pam, "Did Anna tell you everything that Rae said?"

"Who's Rae?" Pam asked.

"Rae is this stuck-up name Rema wants everyone to call her," Anna said.

Pam and Lulu laughed.

"Anna, how can you hate someone you don't even know?" Lulu asked.

"I have a feeling about her. I think she's a — "

" — snob." Pam and Lulu completed the sentence with her.

It seemed to Lulu that Pam was taking forever to turn Lightning around. And Anna was having trouble getting Acorn to stop grazing and get moving. "I'll meet you guys there," Lulu said.

As she ran along the trail at her fastest pace, Lulu was remembering the first time she was on Pony Pal Trail and how she'd wished she had a pony to ride.

When the woods opened up to the paddock, Lulu saw that Snow White was waiting for her. "Snow White!" she called. "Snow White, I've got the best news."

As she ran to Snow White, she saw that the pony had a bit in her mouth and a saddle on her back. Mrs. Crandal was standing nearby holding the reins. "She's strong enough to be ridden now," she said.

"Are you sure?" Lulu asked.

Mrs. Crandal nodded. "For just a short walk. You can go out a little longer each day."

Lulu patted Snow White and said, "I'll

take the best care of you, Snow White. I really will. I love you."

Anna and Acorn and Pam and Lightning came off the trail and stopped near Lulu and Snow White.

Lulu looked up at them. Anna and Pam were grinning from ear to ear. Pam said, "As soon as Anna called with the good news, we went right to the Baxters' to get the tack. That's Rema's — I mean Rae's — saddle and bridle."

Lulu tightened the girth around Snow White's stomach.

"Lulu, do you want me to give you a leg up?" Mrs. Crandal asked.

"I can mount by myself," Lulu said. She put her left foot in the stirrup and in a swift, graceful movement hoisted herself up onto her pony.

She adjusted the stirrups, took proper hold of the reins, and balanced herself in the saddle.

"Snow White is the perfect size for you Lulu," Pam said.

Looking straight ahead between Snow White's alert ears, Lulu saw that they were facing the open gate to Pony Pal Trail.

She took a deep breath, squeezed her calves against Snow White's sides, and said, "Okay, Snow White, let's go for a ride."

Dear Reader:

I am having a lot of fun researching and writing books about the Pony Pals. I've met many interesting kids and adults who love ponies. And I've visited some wonderful ponies at homes, farms, and riding schools.

Before writing Pony Pals I wrote fourteen novels for children and young adults. Four of these were honored by Children's Choice Awards.

I live in Sharon, Connecticut, with my husband, Lee, and our dog, Willie. Our daughter is all grown up and has her own apartment in New York City.

Besides writing novels I like to draw, paint, garden, and swim. I didn't have a pony when I was growing up, but I have always loved them and dreamt about riding. Now I take riding lessons on a horse named Saz.

I like reading and writing about ponies as much as I do riding. Which proves to me that you don't have to ride a pony to love them. And you certainly don't need a pony to be a Pony Pal.

Happy Reading,

Jeanne Betancourt